BUSTER
catches a cold

By Hisako Madokoro   English text by Patricia Lantier   Illustrated by Ken Kuroi

Library of Congress Cataloging-in-Publication Data

Madokoro, Hisako, 1938-
 [Ame no hi no Korowan. English]
 Buster catches a cold / text by Hisako Madokoro ;
illustrations by Ken Kuroi.
  p. cm. — (The Adventures of Buster the puppy)
 Translation of: Ame no hi no Korowan.
 Summary: Buster the puppy ignores his mother's
instructions and goes outside for an adventure in
the rain.
 ISBN 0-8368-0489-9
 [1. Dogs—Fiction. 2. Rain and rainfall—Fiction.]
I. Kuroi, Ken, 1947- ill. II. Title. III. Series:
Madokoro, Hisako, 1938- Korowan. English.
PZ7.M2657Bub 1991
[E]—dc20
                                    90-47948

North American edition first published in 1991 by
Gareth Stevens Children's Books
1555 North RiverCenter Drive, Suite 201
Milwaukee, Wisconsin 53212, USA

This U.S. edition copyright © 1991. Text
copyright © 1991 by Gareth Stevens, Inc. First
published as *Ame No Hi No Korowan* (*Korowan in
the Rain*) in Japan with an original copyright
© 1983 by Hisako Madokoro (text) and Ken Kuroi
(illustrations). English translation rights arranged
with CHILD HONSHA through Japan Foreign-
Rights Centre.

All rights reserved. No part of this book may
be reproduced or used in any form or by any
means without written permission from Gareth
Stevens, Inc.

Cover design: Kristi Ludwig

Printed in the United States of America

    6 7 8 9 97 96 95 94 93

Gareth Stevens Children's Books
MILWAUKEE

2

"Don't go out in the rain, Buster," said his mother. "You'll catch a nasty cold."

4

Buster waited until his
mother was asleep. Then he
tiptoed outside. "I wonder
what a cold is," he thought
to himself.

5

"If I see something that looks
like it might be a cold, I'll
be sure not to catch it,"
he decided.

A frog jumped out of
a flowering bush.
"Yipes!" cried Buster.
"A cold!"

"I'm not a cold," said the
frog. "I'm a frog."

8

"C'mon, let's play tag!"

10

Buster saw a snail on a leaf.
He stood on a stone for a
closer look. "Are you a
cold?" he asked the snail.

13

"Of course I'm not a cold,"
said the snail as he crawled
away through a puddle.

The frog hopped away, too,
and Buster was left alone
in the rain.

"I don't think I'll ever see
a cold!" he thought,
and shivered.

18

Suddenly, Buster saw a
huge puddle in front of him.
"I wonder if colds live in
puddles," he thought.

Buster stared into the water.
Staring back at him was a
terrible face with a big
pink tongue.

"Help!" Buster cried.
"A cold!"

Buster hit the face with his paw and got even wetter himself. "Ah-choo!" sneezed Buster, and he ran for home.

"Ah-choo!   AH-CHOOOO!"

"I said you'd catch a cold,"
said his mother, covering him
with a warm blanket.

"Sorry, Mother," said Buster.
"But I did enjoy the rain.
Ah-choo!"